OUTCASTS

D0231584

For Chiara Stone, who gives me
so much light that it's amazing
she has any left for herself,
for Gem Stone, Daniela Sereno-
Spicer, Rachael Ogden and
Arlene Danton for listening to
my problems ... but especially
for Victoria Jenkins: thank you
for sticking with me as long
as you did.

OUTCASTS

DESTINY

david grimstone

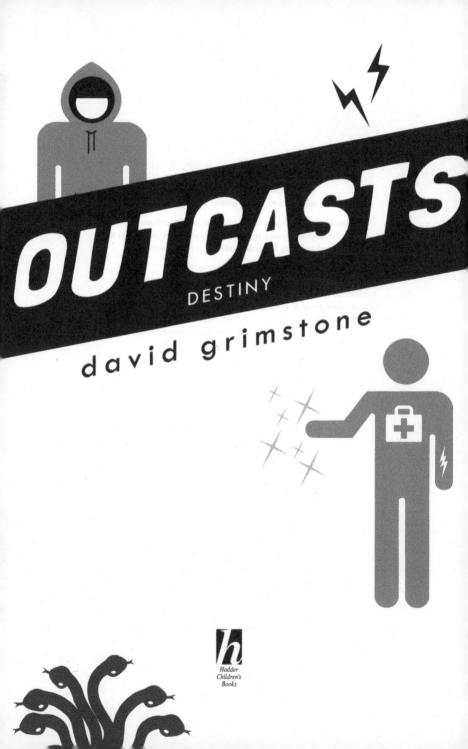

h
Hodder
Children's
Books

HODDER CHILDREN'S BOOKS

First published in Great Britain in 2017 by Hodder and Stoughton

1 3 5 7 9 10 8 6 4 2

Text copyright © David Grimstone, 2017
Inside illustrations © Shutterstock

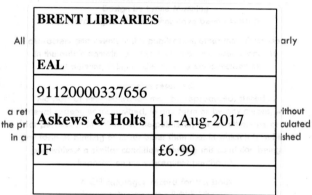

BRENT LIBRARIES		
EAL		
91120000337656		
Askews & Holts	11-Aug-2017	
JF	£6.99	

All ... arly

a ret ... ithout
the pr ... culated
in a ... ished

ISBN 978 1 444 92539 5

Printed and bound in Great Britain by
Clays Ltd, St Ives plc

The paper and board used in this book
are made from wood from responsible sources.

MIX
Paper from
responsible sources
FSC® C104740

Hodder Children's Books
An imprint of
Hachette Children's Group
Part of Hodder and Stoughton
Carmelite House
50 Victoria Embankment
London EC4Y 0DZ

An Hachette UK Company
www.hachette.co.uk

www.hachettechildrens.co.uk

PREVIOUSLY IN
OUTCASTS

When school friends Jake, Fatyak, Lemon and Kellogg happen upon a mysterious box during a game of Darkness & Destiny, they have no idea that they're venturing into a world of magic and mayhem. Suddenly, each Outcast is imbued with special powers, but these come at a price. Pursued by The Reach, a supposed government agency that was charged with protecting Pandora's Box, they find themselves hunted like animals, until a grim confrontation leaves them with more power and responsibility than they could ever have bargained for.

CONTENTS

1

Bad Signs

Despite the fact that they were wearing immaculate suits while the hundred or so gamers in the room were all decked out in baggy cargo pants and t-shirts, the two men were moving around Butter's game shop as if they were invisible.

Rufus Tern, who was dealing Uno cards for The Outcasts in a distracted fashion, only noticed the pair when they actually asked him to move his chair in order to let them pass.

'Who are they?' Jake asked, as the table was tipped slightly to afford their passage.

'Estate Agents,' Lemon growled, accidentally cracking the table when she leaned her elbow on it. 'Ooops, I think I broke something.' She put a hand over the damage. 'The Butter family can sell this place now that Stew has been missing for – what – over a year?'

'Since we lost the Box, in fact. I still say The Reach took him.'

Jake and Rufus shook their heads sadly, but Kellogg's distracted gaze was fixed on the first card that had been positioned in the middle of the table after Rufus had dealt all the hands and the others were picking up their decks.

'You can't START Uno with a plus four,' he said, frowning.

Lemon squinted at the cards, and shrugged. 'Why not? I've got two plus fours in my hand, so I'm okay.'

'Me too,' said Jake.

'And me,' Rufus admitted.

Kellogg rolled his eyes.

'Er ... that's insane? If you've all got two plus fours, it means I'm going to have to pick up twenty-four cards before I even get a chance to play!'

'So?'

'SO ... I'm going to have a hand

with, like, thirty-five cards in it. I can't even HOLD thirty-five cards.'

Jake smiled. 'I thought you were a superhero?' he said.

The Outcasts burst out laughing, but this quickly died away as the smirk on Jake's face gave way to a pained expression.

'Still bad?' Rufus asked, a worried edge to his voice. 'I thought you lot were getting better?'

'We're getting more powerful,' Kellogg admitted, with a concerned frown. 'But the pain is getting worse. It's as if the two things grow together.

'I don't want to talk about it.'

Lemon glanced around her: despite the large crowd of gamers in the shop, there *did* seem to be slightly fewer players in recent weeks. 'I'm sad about this place. Maybe people are playing the games here, but buying them somewhere else?' she said. 'Or, you know, just hitting their consoles instead?'

'I can't believe it might close down, but I'm more worried about you guys,' Rufus said, dragging them back to reality. 'When you say your powers are growing, what do you mean? You're not going to explode or anything, are you?'

Jake shrugged, nervously. 'I can conjure ANYTHING now and I know

Lemon is stronger than ever. But we're both suffering, physically. The pain is slow, constant and exhausting. Kellogg, can you do something?'

The scrawny youth nodded, placed a hand each over the wrists of his two friends and closed his eyes.

As Rufus looked on, a bright yellow glow began to seep into their flesh.

'Only two days, this time,' Kellogg muttered, as he gave strength to the pair. 'You're needing more and more energy to keep the pain away. We HAVE to find the source of the Box's power. And QUICKLY.'

'You're right,' Jake nodded,

breaking contact and turning over the second card on the main Uno deck to force a fairer start. 'Where's Fatyak, by the way? I know he's always late, but an hour is rido*nkulus*.'

As Kellogg sat back to rejuvenate, the others lapsed into fits of giggles, but Rufus stopped laughing when he realised that Lemon was waiting on him for some sort of answer.

'Why are you looking at me?'

'You were the one who went round to his house at the weekend,' she pointed out. 'Did he mention he was going to be late?'

Rufus stared blankly at them

before a slow light seemed to dawn in his eyes.

'Oh ... RIGHT! Yeah, I dropped by, but they'd gone away. There was a note on his front door. I was a bit miffed that he hadn't bothered to text me first.'

Lemon, Kellogg and Jake said nothing, but carefully laid their cards down on the table.

'Fatyak wouldn't go away without telling us,' Lemon said. 'Especially not with Colonel Bleach on the loose. He's The Reach's top agent, remember? We know they hate Fatyak because he destroyed the box *and* he pushed Bleach over the edge in that sewer drop. I'm amazed they haven't made their move before now. Kellogg has the THUNDERBOLT, after all. That has to be one of their most powerful weapons.'

'It's actually more like a *lightning bolt* ...'

'Who cares? We need to MOVE!'

Jake was already reaching for his backpack. 'We need to get to Fatyak's house,' he said. 'NOW!'

'But it's on the other side of town.' Kellogg moaned, feeling guilty for the fact that he couldn't summon enough energy to sustain himself.

'It is a mission to get over there,' Lemon admitted. 'I'd ask mum and dad to drive us but they're in London at a conference. Again.'

Jake smiled sympathetically. 'We'll take the bus,' he said. 'We haven't done that for ages.'

2

Old Enemies

Historically, there were a number of reasons why The Outcasts never used public transport. These included the fact that none of them could understand the bus and train timetables. Even Kellogg claimed he could read them easily, but always got them wrong. Although, the biggest reason was because the bus had always been the weekend hangout of class bully Todd Miller and his odious gang.

Admittedly, the rumour mill had been suggesting that Miller and his horrible girlfriend had recently split up and that Todd's groupies had left with her, but you could never hedge your bets when it came to the dreaded 'TM'. Still, Lemon assured the group that her last run-in with the senior had been so colossally bad for him that they should all feel safe in any of his usual haunts.

'Ten minutes,' Kellogg said, studying the timetable while running his finger up one column and down the other. 'No, fifteen. Wait ... no, it's twenty minutes. Yeah: every twenty minutes. So ... er ...'

'Just tell us when the next one will

be along,' Lemon muttered, irritably.

Kellogg checked his watch. 'Not for another fifteen minutes,' he said, just as a bus pulled into the stop. 'Oh. Right. *Now I get it.*'

Jake pushed in front and they all trouped onto the bus, immediately feeling self-conscious when they saw the vehicle was packed full of kids, with a few miserable looking Saturday shoppers dotted in between them.

'Four to the High School stop,' Jake said, handing over a ten-pound note while the others looked around for somewhere to sit.

'We'll have to stand,' said Kellogg,

sullenly.

'I can't,' Rufus warned. 'I get really sick from all the swaying. Look! There's a whole bench free up at the back, but ... Oh. Maybe not.'

Todd Miller was sitting on his own on the seats at the very end of the bus. His reputation had ensured that the other four spaces remained vacant.

'Come on,' Lemon said, confidently. 'We need to sit down and there are four empty seats right there.'

Without uttering another word, she strode purposefully towards the back of the bus, the others trailing slowly behind her.

Todd Miller spotted the group before they got anywhere near the back seat, but contrary to all traditional expectations, he straightened himself up and stared directly ahead of him — his eyes so fixed on the seat in front of him that it looked as though he was some sort of android.

The Outcasts nervously filed onto the step and took their seats on the big couch, Jake in the opposite corner to Miller with Kellogg and Rufus filling the spaces next to him.

Lemon took the seat beside Miller.

'Hey Todd,' she said, in what she hoped was a friendly, conversational tone. 'How are things going with you?'

Miller turned his head so slowly that he might have been wearing a neck brace.

'D-don't hit my face,' he said.

Lemon frowned. 'What?'

'I-if you're going to attack me, please leave my face clear. My parents have a big fundraising party tonight and I'm supposed to be ...'

'Why would I hit you?' Lemon barked, so suddenly that Miller actually winced and shrank back from her. 'You haven't done anything ... today.'

'P-please just leave m-me alone.'

The Outcasts shared confused

glances as Lemon, evidently irritated by the bully's unusual reaction, tried to press her point.

'I only asked you how you were doing today.'

'My stop!' Miller shouted as he jumped up and almost toppled over the seat in front. Snatching hold of the rail, he frantically pressed the stop button, ringing the bell over and over as he scrambled across the hastily unoccupied seat in order to reach the aisle.

Glancing back once in order to make sure he wasn't being followed by The Outcasts, he half ran, half tripped his way off the bus, making the final jump onto the street with such a frantic leap that he was still midair when the bus took off again.

The Outcasts erupted into fits of laughter, but Lemon just glared at them, her face red with fury.

'We have to get rid of these powers,' she snapped, as the laughter died away. 'Look what they've turned us into.'

'What?' Kellogg frowned. 'What have they turned us into?'

'HIM.'

Lemon took in the baleful stares of her friends, but her expression remained frozen. 'I'm serious. If we're not careful, we're going to end up becoming the very things we set out to stand against.'

3

Ransacked!

Fatyak lived midway along a small row of terraced cottages, a short distance from the high school. The Reed family house stood out a mile because Fatyak's mum didn't have enough money to get the front painted. The entire property looked as though it had just been teleported in from the 1980s.

'What if The Reach are watching the place?' Kellogg muttered. 'We should be careful.'

Lemon rolled her eyes. 'Considering that Jake can conjure stuff out of thin air, I can rip trees from the grounds and you have a lightning bolt in your arm, shouldn't *they* be hiding from *us*?'

Kellogg pushed in front. 'I agree. Let's just go and see Fatyak, shall we?'

Jake shrugged. 'Fine. Whatever.'

Lemon strode boldly up to Fatyak's door and hammered on it several times before standing back and looking up expectantly at the front of the house.

While she waited, Kellogg peered

into the living room window that bordered the street, cupping his hands over his eyes in an effort to block out the blinding sunlight. Beyond the pane, he could just make out the familiar arrangement in Fatyak's living room, with the three sofas and the coffee table all positioned in front of the TV. Everything looked normal.

Lemon was just about to step away from Fatyak's house when there was a loud click and the front door swung open.

All three Outcasts stared at Rufus with a look of disbelief.

'What?' said the young boy, resentfully. 'I saw Fatyak's mum grab a key from under the flowerpot when we came round for that pizza night. Are you coming in or what?'

The three friends piled into the hallway, hurriedly shutting the door behind them.

'I'm pretty sure this is breaking and entering,' Kellogg warned. 'Just saying.'

'Rubbish!' Lemon argued. 'How is it breaking? Rufus had the key. It might be "entering" but I'm not certain that's an actual crime.'

'Er, hello? Trespassing?' Kellogg just stared at her.

'Oh, yeah. I guess.'

They moved from room to room, making a cursory inspection of the house without touching anything. All made an unspoken effort not to disturb the furnishings or leave any noticeable marks on the carpet.

'Everything seems the same,' Jake admitted. 'It just doesn't look that tidy, you know.'

'It's never tidy,' Lemon pointed out. 'You *have* been round here before, right?'

'Yeah, but people usually clean up a bit when they're leaving for a holiday. Look at all the pizza boxes!'

Kellogg opened one of the extra-large cardboard containers and grimaced. 'Eugh. My last ham and pineapple slice is still in here, we've had four sleepovers since then!'

'Gross!'

Lemon grinned, shook her head in despair. 'Shall we look upstairs?'

Trailing after Rufus, the group reached the first floor landing and went off in separate directions, each checking a different room.

'Nothing in here!' Lemon called, from the main bedroom.

'Bathroom's clear,' Jake added.

'In HERE!'

The shout had come from Rufus, who was in Fatyak's bedroom or, at least, what was left of it.

A shattered window was the least

disturbing sight in an absolute maelstrom of chaos. The computer looked as if it had been hurled at the wall, as the file-server lay in two parts at the foot of Fatyak's bed while the monitor had come to rest on top of a toy chest, a deep crack running along the length of the screen.

The bed had been tipped on its side and it looked like a knife blade had been used to tear open the bottom of the mattress. The wardrobe had been wrenched away from the wall and largely dismantled, while the chest of drawers had practically been returned to its original flat-pack components.

'What the hell?' Kellogg muttered

as he avoided stepping on a patch of broken glass. 'Look at this place, it's wrecked.'

'It's obvious they were after something specific,' Rufus said, peering at the devastated mattress. 'Do you think they're looking for the lightning bolt?'

'In a mattress?' Jake frowned. 'If they are, their detective skills are on the wane!'

'I just don't think they took Fatyak.'

All eyes turned to Lemon, who had moved to stand beside the shattered window.

Jake frowned at her. 'Why do you think that?'

'Well,' she said, stepping away from the window and nodding towards the street. 'Unlike all those not very suspicious people out front, the guy in the van on the road behind the alley is *definitely* a Reach Agent. I don't know why he'd be parked up there if they'd already taken Fatyak prisoner.'

Jake glared out at the van, and cracked his knuckles.

'It's one of the pair that hit Lemon's house the night the box was destroyed,' he spat. 'Let's just hope Nathan Heed isn't out of prison, too. I don't fancy going up against that poisonous little snake again.'

Lemon grinned. 'Look, the moron in

the van isn't paying attention, so he won't see us coming. This is it. This time, they *don't* get away.'

Jake raced to the door, but was practically snatched out of the air by Lemon, who hauled him off his feet and drove him against the wall of the room.

'Lem? What the hell are you doing?'

Holding Jake firmly with one strong hand, she raised a finger to her lips and rolled her eyes upwards. 'The roof,' she whispered, as a dull, repetitive thud became audible from the ceiling. 'I think there's someone on the roof.'

Rufus froze, while Kellog made his way to the window.

Fatyak's bedroom was part of a first floor loft extension that gave the impression of being a later addition to the house. It had a low, flat ash felt roof that sloped away from the top of the house.

'It's just a seagull,' Kellogg whispered. 'I've stayed in this room before. Those birds sound massive when they first land ...'

Jake shook his head. Admittedly, it had gone extremely quiet since they had stopped talking in loud voices.

'Kellogg,' he said in a low, deliberate voice. 'You, Lemon and Rufus go see to that idiot in the van. I'm going to check out the roof.'

While the others flooded out of the bedroom, Jake moved through the house to the small set of attic steps that led up into the loft conversion. Tackling the stairs, which were almost vertical, he dragged himself into the attic, crossed over to the window and carefully climbed out onto the roof. A quick glance at the now-deserted street below told him that although levitation was a definite option, he might be seen by neighbours peering from windows up and down the line of terraces.

Grabbing the edge of the slate roof, he brought his knee up and pulled himself onto the overhanging arch of the window. Then he quietly slithered over the slates, working his way toward the chimney stack.

He was halfway there when he saw a figure in a hooded tracksuit, crouching low against the brickwork, a shortwave radio held in front of its face.

'Anything?' it muttered.

'Nothing, boss,' came the crackling reply. 'When's the next shift. Only, I've been here ages and I don't think the fat boy's going to come back here ...'

'STAY WHERE YOU ARE. There are voices coming from the bedroom. I think it's the rest of the gang. Do nothing until you hear from me. We'll deal with them when we've got the pork chop. It was HIM who smashed Pandora's Box, remember?'

This time, Jake immediately recognised a voice that could only belong to Nathan Heed and steeled himself for a fight. He was just about to make the first move when The Reach lieutenant jumped and craned his neck to see around the chimney stack, almost dropping the radio.

'GOT HIM,' he snarled into the device. 'On the street you've parked the van in, third rooftop along from the right. I *told* you he'd come back for his mother.'

'Should I move the van, guv?'

'NO! Stay put. I'll get him myself.'

Heed stashed the radio and raised himself up, moving around the chimney stack in an awkward gait that almost made him slip several times.

Following the direction of his movement, Jake looked across the street to a roof where the distinctive shape of Fatyak detached itself from a similar chimney and crept along the narrow space, deftly leaping over a gap between two neighbouring buildings.

'Okay, boy,' Heed muttered to himself. 'Let's see how fast you really are.'

He reached out with one hand and

mumbled a few words.

To Jake's astonishment, a glowing strand of yellowish cord sprang from Heed's fingers and through the air.

In the distance, Fatyak was moving faster than ever, but he simply didn't see the airborne snare closing in on him. It caught the large boy, mid-jump, wrapping around his ankles and sending him crashing onto a low, flat roof at the edge of the small row of terraces.

'Got you,' Heed yapped, producing the radio once more but this time switching a button on the dial. 'Slud, do you hear me?'

Crackle, crackle.

'Yes, boss. Just leaving the manor.'

'Good. Bring the BIG truck.'

'You got the boy?'

'We might be considerably luckier than that. We might have ALL of them.' He turned to head back for the safety of the chimney stack.

Jake Cherish was blocking his path.

'I see your magical abilities have lingered, Heed,' Jake said, raising himself up and folding his arms. 'I assume that's how you got out of prison, you rotten little worm.' He smiled, enjoying the shocked expression on The Reach agent's twisted face. 'You know, considering that you must be suffering the side effects like us,

I'm surprised Bleach let you off the lead. You know, with the beating we gave you the last time.'

Heed gritted his teeth and sent a cone of cold energy swirling towards Jake, who obliterated it with a wild arc of fire.

'I noticed you haven't managed to master my abilities,' he laughed. 'Hope you've had better luck copying the others.'

Conscious of the fact that they were both risking public display, Jake leaped for The Reach agent. Employing a small amount of magic to increase his velocity, he collided with the little man, convulsing with shock as Heed plucked him out of the air and slammed him bodily onto the slate roof.

Stunned by the strength of Heed's defence, Jake tried and failed to roll over.

'As a matter of fact,' Heed growled. 'I think I've adapted quite well to your friend *Lemon's* particular mould.' He glanced a boot off Jake's face, dazing the boy. 'Thanks for the concern. I'll be back to collect you when I've retrieved your *fat* little friend.'

He half stepped, half tripped across the tiles but made a sizeable jump onto a lower roof.

Still shocked by the onslaught, Jake forced himself up, first onto his elbows and then back to his knees. Looking down at the street, he saw Heed heading towards the place where Fatyak fell. Then he glanced up the road to where The Outcasts were closing in on the white van.

Jake let out a deep, heavy breath and launched himself into the air, roaring away like a missile.

4

Attack!

Clax yawned. He'd been sitting in his van and watching the house for what seemed like five hundred years without receiving the slightest sign that it had even been occupied, let alone that Fatyak, the boy they'd been sent to capture, had risked returning. Now, just when things had finally started to happen, he'd been ordered to stay put and do *nothing*. Of course, he reminded himself, none of this nonsense would have been necessary had Slud not botched the kidnapping in the first place.

He sighed and slumped back in his seat. It was amazing how much trouble one snot-nosed, overweight kid could have caused them, but Colonel Bleach and the powers that be certainly had it in for the boy. Fortunately, the reason behind all this was beyond Clax's pay grade. And he was just fine with that.

He closed his hand over another weary yawn and, trying to think of a way to keep himself awake, switched the van's multi-channel radio to the local police frequency. After a few minutes, he found some moderately interesting chatter and began, very slowly, to relax.

He switched on his mobile phone and reached for the packet of crisps he'd stashed for convenience in the glove compartment. Unfortunately, he'd only just put the first one into his mouth when he glanced through the windscreen and spat it out again.

Two of The Outcasts were running up the road towards the van.

Clax blinked when he saw the girl, *the horrible,* ridiculously tough girl from the catastrophic battle in the house.

His mind raced, but his body reacted to the mountain of cowardice that dwarfed his inner courage. He slammed his foot on the accelerator and drove the van towards the group.

'Go wide,' Kellogg said, running so fast that he could just about summon a breath. 'The others might be in the back.'

As they ran, Clax put his foot down and the van lurched forward, its wheels spinning.

'Kellogg! DODGE!'

The skinny youth dived aside, but Lemon leaped onto the front of the van, a grim expression on her face. She snatched hold of the windscreen wipers as the truck swerved onto the road. When she saw Claxon's demented face behind the windscreen, a terrible recognition flashed in her eyes.

Clax floored the pedal so hard that the truck began to gain momentum, the engine screaming at the vehicle roared for the end of the street.

'Kellogg!' Lemon yelled. 'Get on! QUICKLY!'

Scrambling onto his feet, Kellogg ran at his top speed, leaping onto the back of the van and stretching out an arm to Rufus, who appeared from the mouth of an alley and put on an impressive burst of energy in order to catch up.

After a frantic few seconds during which their fingers entirely failed to meet and entwine, Rufus managed a desperate leap to reach his friend's outstretched gasp. He was dragged on board the speeding van.

'Where's Fatyak?' Lemon screamed as the van raced through the streets, drawing the shocked attention of several pedestrians as it hurtled towards the edge of town. She reached back with a balled fist to smash the glass. 'Have you got him in there? Have you? Let's take a look!'

Claxon yanked on the steering wheel, sending the van off down a new street that appeared to terminate at the outer wall of a community park.

Lemon gripped the windscreen so

hard that her knuckles flushed white.

Behind the wheel of the vehicle, Clax swore loudly, his eyes bulging as he peered around the girl on the windscreen at the wall racing towards him.

He slammed on the breaks, and Lemon flew back onto the road. She landed awkwardly, rolling over backwards and ending her journey on the edge of the pavement. As she struggled to her feet, Claxon roared forward again, but she dived aside and the van jumped the pavement, narrowly avoiding several garden walls as it swerved around in a wild arc, sending Rufus and Kellogg in different directions.

Lemon was on the vehicle even before it screeched to a halt, snatching hold of the side door-handle and wrenching on the lock until it snapped and the door slid open.

Claxon shifted the truck into reverse, but as he tried to back it up, Lemon snatched hold of his collar and dragged him into the shadowy depths of the van.

Scrambling to hold onto every fixture and fitting on the way, Claxon wriggled free from the girl's iron grip, ripping his coat in the process. He threw two closed fists at Lemon, but she blocked them both and snapped her head forward with such force that the blow knocked Claxon through the open door of the truck. He hit the road in a crumpled heap, groaning a few times, before he managed to get back onto his knees.

Lemon reached down, snatched hold of Claxon's collar and lifted him bodily off the ground.

The big man twisted weakly and tried to throw his arm out but Lemon knocked it side as if she was reprimanding a small child.

'P-please,' he spat. 'No more, no MORE!'

'What are you here for?' she

demanded, grabbing his nose with her free hand and twisting it. 'Where's Fatyak? Tell us!'

'I dunno! I swear! We ambushed the family over the weekend, tried to grab your big mate but he got away. We snatched his mother instead, took her as leverage. I was sent back here to see if he showed up!'

'Sent by who? Bleach?'

'N-nathan Heed! He-he was up on the roof, b-back a the house—'

'NATHAN HEED?' Lemon frowned, then a smile twisted her face into a series of dark shadows. 'Out of prison, is he?'

'Y-yeah.'

'Where are you holding Fatyak's mum?' she growled, twisting his nasal appendage until there was a crack.

'Arghh! ARGHH!'

'Talk now, or I'll just ... keep ... twisting.'

'The Big House!'

'Where?'

'Drake Mansion! Edge of Crowford! I swear! It's where we all get our orders from!'

'Liar! You get your orders from COLONEL BLEACH!'

'Yeah, but even Bleach gets instructions from the mansion.'

Lemon nodded, and dragged

his face close to her lips. 'I'm going to put you to sleep now,' she growled, 'it's nothing personal, but we might need you and your van a bit later on. I'll make it quick.'

As she used her powers to gain control, Rufus and Kellogg staggered over to join her, both nursing cuts and bruises attained in their flight from the van. Kellogg was already attempting to heal the damage: a shimmering green light had spilled from his fingers to envelop both he and Rufus in a soothing emerald glow. Lemon looked down at Clax and bared her teeth at the henchman. 'They've taken Fatyak's mum,' she said, darkly, 'but this idiot claims Bleach gets his instructions from a place called Drake Manor. I guess that's where we need to go. AFTER we've found Fatyak.'

'We're not going after Fatyak,' said a voice.

Jake Cherish floated to the ground, a grim look on his face.

'What?' Lemon frowned. 'Didn't you hear what ...'

'I heard everything.'

'But ...'

'I just ran into Nathan Heed and came off worse,' Jake admitted. 'As much as I want to help Fatyak, we'll have more chance of saving him *and his mum* if we confront whoever's actually in charge of The Reach. If you believe this thug about the manor ...'

'Er, I do.' Rufus fished in his pocket and, flushing red, produced a familiar-looking mobile phone. 'It's Fatyak's,' he said. 'I found it in the conservatory on the way out. The last five messages were all to us, but none of them delivered. Something must have been blocking his signal.'

Jake frowned. 'What did they say?'

Rufus held up the handset. The display read:

Lemon nodded. 'Great. Fatyak

Reach watching Kellogg

am following them

massive place – edge of Crowford

think they saw me

watch ur backs

was tailing The Reach and they ended up grabbing his poor mum.'

'It's my fault,' said Kellogg sullenly. 'It's all my fault. They want the lightning bolt and I ...'

'Don't start that,' Jake warned him. 'There's no blame to place here. We knew this was coming. There's us and there's them and now it's war.'

'Let's look on the bright side,' Lemon added. 'We've got transport and a driver who knows exactly where to go. Don't worry, he's a total idiot.'

'Perfect,' Jake nodded. 'Lemon, can you or Rufus start calling around, let the folks know everyone is staying at my place tonight.'

'Huh?'

'We can't hit the mansion in daylight. If Drake Mansion really is The Reach HQ, they'll have eagle eyes on any unexpected approach. We need to wait until nightfall.'

Rufus nodded. 'Fine. I'll handle it.'

'Great. Kellogg, can you use your healing vibes to wake him up, so he's in a state to drive?'

'I had to knock him out,' Lemon admitted. 'Found the cuffs in the back. I've got the key. If Kellogg can work his magic, the guy should be fit to drive us to Drake Manor.'

Jake opened the front door of the van. 'Where *is* Drake Manor?'

'It's the big house out beyond Farm Hill Road,' Rufus said. 'The one with the circular drive and those gates with the two weird squatting gargoyles on them.'

Kellogg appeared at the side of the van, dragging Claxon with him.

'Drake Manor,' Lemon growled at the cowering thug, 'and, remember, if we get stopped by the police, *you're* the one going to jail for breaking and entering, assault on a minor *and* kidnapping.'

5

Night Raid

The manor was in darkness as the van chugged up the hill towards it. The one shattered headlight offering the only illumination on the road.

There wasn't a single light visible in the two great rows of windows that crowded the face of the sprawling house and the great drive was devoid of cars.

Inside the van, Jake, otherwise known as Dealmo was sitting quietly with his knees tucked up to his chest, while

Kellogg messed around with the lightning bolt. He'd discovered that if he closed his fist, the bolt shrank away completely and it was like being empty-handed until he stretched out his fingers. At this point, the shaped lightning spread out and grew once again.

Rufus watched the display silently, his jaw dropping at regular intervals.

Lemon commanded Clax to bring the van to a halt a short distance from the entrance gates before chaining the brute to the side door once again.

Then The Outcasts slowly made their way to the gates on foot. Lemon reached up to press the intercom, but a hand closed over her wrist before she could activate the switch.

'Dealmo? What is it?'

Jake, who hadn't spoken more than a few words since the group had left Fatyak's house, was staring at the house and shaking his head.

'I have a bad feeling about this,' he muttered. 'I don't know enough about my magical *gift* to say whether I'm just scared or whether I'm getting some sort of psychic warning, but I really don't think we should go in there. I get the feeling there's something dangerous ...'

'More dangerous than us?'

'Well, actually, yes.'

Lemon looked annoyed. 'This is where we might finally get an answer, Dealmo. This is where we could find out why we feel sick and tired all the time, why we have these incredible powers and what the cost is to our bodies! Please tell me you're not chickening out? You're supposed to be our *leader*, remember? Besides, you're basically a wizard, I punch holes in walls and Kellogg has a lightning bolt quite literally *up his sleeve*. How bad can our enemies really be?'

Jake looked down at his feet, but it was Kellogg who spoke.

'The whole place is in darkness,' he said. 'That's a bit odd, isn't it?. If you live in a house that big, you leave lights and stuff on when you go out and you probably have servants. Yet it looks sort of abandoned.'

'So what?' Lemon rolled her eyes. 'If it's a trap, let's spring it. Rufus is the only one with a genuine reason to be scared, and he isn't saying *anything*, are you Rufus?' She glanced around. 'Rufus?'

They peered around them, but – apart from the van half hidden beside the road – the area was completely deserted. Rufus was nowhere to be seen.

'Great!' Kellogg muttered, irritably. 'Where's he gone now? I knew we shouldn't have brought him along with us!'

The group began to fan out, casting glances in all directions until Kellogg finally spotted Rufus on the crest of a nearby hill.

'Hey!' Jake called, trying to muffle the shout. 'What are you doing up there?'

The boy hurried back down the hill, pointing at the road as he ran.

'Get down!' he cried. 'There's something coming along the road!'

They looked back at the house, Lemon ducking her head while Jake and Kellogg actively hit the ground.

A haulage truck appeared at the bottom of Farm Hill Road, headlights streaming in the distance. The noise it made seemed to shake Jake from his reverie.

'Okay,' he said, turning to Lemon. 'Can you bend the bars on the fence?'

Lemon shrugged, and moved towards the gate.

'Not here!' Jake whispered. 'Come on. We're going round the back.'

They moved through the undergrowth and skirted the perimeter of the estate, but as they reached a slight rise on the western edge of the fence, Kellogg realised the noise of the truck had become louder and he glanced back towards the road.

'That truck stopped at the gates,' he

said, squinting into the middle distance.

'So?'

'So who gets a delivery late at night?'

'Shh! Look! Jake, get over here! And you two!'

Lemon dragged Rufus and Kellogg close to the edge of the fence and pointed towards the house, where an eerie green glow had suddenly illuminated a low, flat construct a short way from the main building. It looked like a pool house, judging from the shadow of the water playing clearly across the ceiling. The emerald shimmer moved from window to window, becoming the outline of a girl in some sort of flowing gown and a strange headdress. She was followed by two other shadows that seemed to lengthen behind her as she moved towards the ornate glass door that led out onto the gardens.

Jake gave Lemon a nudge. 'Quick! Let's get in before they see us!'

Lemon nodded, reached for the bars at the side of the fence and began, very slowly, to pull them apart. They widened with a low, distinct creak, and she climbed inside. Dealmo followed, but Kellogg was more hesitant. The gangly youth was still looking towards the front of the house, where the gate had been opened and the entire courtyard was bathed in the truck's twin headlights.

'Th-that's Nathan Heed!' he said, suddenly, straining to see through the shadows. 'I'd recognise that face anywhere. I've been seeing it in my nightmares since the fight in Lemon's garden last year. Colonel Bleach is with him, too! They're coming this way, and it looks like they've got company!'

Lemon gritted her teeth. 'Just means we're in the right place,' she said, dragging Kellogg and Rufus through the bars. 'Let's move!'

The group moved quickly across the open ground, heading for the low building. As they moved closer to the manor, a series of floodlights flashed on all over the grounds, casting such brilliant points of clarity on the side of the manor that they could have all been standing in daylight.

'What is this place?'

The courtyard they could now see was full of strangely carved statues, all arranged to form what looked like a sort of artistic diorama. Despite the beauty of the arrangement, the scene was extremely chilling.

Rufus stopped dead approximately halfway across the courtyard, his frown slowly developing into a look of horrified fascination.

'Isn't that …'

'Rufus! Come on!'

Lemon, Kellogg and Jake were all beckoning impatiently at the boy, darting glances between the house and the truck in order to make sure they stayed undetected.

'What are you doing?' Jake prompted.

'It's HER,' Rufus said, pointing a shaking finger at the nearest statue. 'It's Fatyak's mum.'

'What?' Lemon stared, open-mouthed, at the stone figure.

'Oh, don't be ridiculous,' said Kellogg, dismissively. 'It's a statue, dude.

Get real!'

'It's a statue of Fatyak's mum,' Rufus repeated, his voice full of quiet terror.

Lemon and Kellogg both gawped at the statue, but Jake stepped forward and leaned really close to the stone.

'It is,' he said, his voice sounding suddenly distant. 'It *is* Fatyak's mum: why would they make a statue of her?'

He moved sideways in order to take a closer look at some of the others.

'Stew,' he muttered, putting his hand on another statue. 'Stew Butter from the game shop! He sold us the box, remember?'

'Er, these are just statues, right?'

Kellogg said, his nervous laughter making them all feel distinctly uneasy. 'They're not the *actual* people?'

Jake, Rufus and Lemon all stared at the diorama of stone faces.

'H-how could they be?' Lemon asked. 'I mean, what sort of monster could do this to a person?'

'A basilisk could,' said Rufus, who knew a lot about monsters and mythology. 'Either that or a gorgon. Medusa was a gorgon and she could turn people to stone with a single glance.'

'I think if Medusa still existed, we'd have heard about it,' said Kellogg.

'Really?' Jake shrugged. 'Did you

hear anything about Pandora's Box before we found it on a shelf in a game shop?'

'Quick!' Lemon whispered. 'There's no time for a big discussion! Heed and Bleach are on their way round the side of the house! In here! NOW! It's open!'

She'd found a low door into the smaller building and was holding it ajar.

'Wide open with no alarm?' Jake glanced at Kellogg and shook his head before heading through the door to be faced with whatever might lie within.

6

Drake Manor

The group found themselves at one end of a luxurious looking swimming pool that threw a series of beautiful reflections onto the low roof.

'Look at this place,' Kellogg whispered. 'How much does it cost to have a pool like that? There's even a tunnel under the water!'

'It leads outside,' Rufus observed, remembering the narrow pool he'd noticed cutting across the courtyard.

'Major security risk, if you ask me.'

'This way,' Jake said, confidently. 'That door up ahead looks like it connects to the main house, and I'm guessing it will be unlocked, because someone *wanted* us to get in here.'

He reached the door and, sure enough, it yawned open. The corridor beyond lead to a long hall with high ceilings, cluttered with suits of armour and more of the strangely unappealing statues they'd seen earlier in the garden.

As they moved along the hall, Jake firmly in the lead, a door opened and closed from somewhere at the front of the house. A series of weird echoes followed the sound.

Arriving at a junction, Jake looked both ways, seeing rows of different doors in each direction. On a whim, he went right but ignored the many choices on offer, choosing instead to go for the door at the far end of the hall.

It led into a small, rectangular room that looked like a miniature art gallery designed by some wild eccentric. The chessboard floor sloped sharply downwards, making the arrangement of furniture seem like an impossible feat at first glance. It was only on closer inspection that it became apparent that every armchair had been secured in place. There were a number of cruelly ripped holes in the ceiling, each granting passage to a network of thick vines that hung down from the floor above.

'I played a level like this in Thief on the Xbox,' said Rufus, trying to make light of his own nervous apprehension.

'This place is really *weird*,' Jake agreed, 'and not in a good way. I could swear those portraits are moving.'

Rufus and Kellogg glanced at the walls, both immediately drawn to a large framed painting of an old man in a flowing ceremonial gown with some sort of temple in the background. He looked self-possessed, sporting a smile that managed to be magnanimous and oddly threatening at the same time. He was holding ...

'A lightning bolt,' Kellogg observed, glancing from the painting to his own shaking hand. 'Just like the one I have.'

'It's Zeus,' Rufus confirmed, leaning forward to take a closer look. 'I've never seen him painted like that, though. I guess the background is supposed to be a temple on Mount Olympus. It's incredibly realistic, isn't it? My mum showed me all the Zeus paintings in the museum's restoration room, but he looked a lot *kinder* in those.'

'He's got some muscles on him,' said Kellogg. 'I reckon even Lemon would have a hard job arm wrestling him.'

He turned to glance at Lemon, but she was otherwise occupied with a painting on the far side of the room.

Jake, meanwhile, had become fascinated by an entirely different portrait, showing a young boy in the same sort of garb standing on the side of a lonely mountain path. A mist curled around the boy's feet, giving the impression that he was floating rather than standing.

'I don't like the look of this kid,' Jake admitted, trying to work out if the glow around the edge of the painting was simply the result of the spotlight fixed above it. 'Do you think he's a god, too?'

'Might be Hermes,' Kellogg said, stepping back to glance at the picture Jake was staring at. 'I don't know much about Greek gods, but I'm pretty sure he wore winged boots, and that boy looks like he's hovering off the ground.'

'Um ...' Rufus had turned away from the portraits and was focusing his own worried glance on the far side of the room, where Lemon now stood in front of a smaller picture, her expression vacant and her arms hanging loosely by her sides. She wasn't moving. 'What's wrong with Lemon?'

Jake and Kellogg both approached the girl from different sides, their eyes immediately finding the strange picture that had provoked such a strong reaction from their friend.

The portrait was stunning, partly because the young woman depicted in it was strikingly beautiful, but mostly because there was an emerald sheen to her eyes that made them seem to glance out at you from the surface of the painting. Jake had seen an effect like this before, when his parents had taken him to the Louvre. The Mona Lisa had a deceptive gaze that gave the impression she was following your progress around the room.

'Don't look at her,' he warned, as Rufus and Kellogg drew in.

'What?'

'Eh?'

'The girl in the picture,' he barked. 'Don't look at her. I'm serious! This room is really creepy and I think there's something magical going on here. All my senses are tingling and I have this pain like there's somebody inside my head with me.' He put a hand on Lemon's arm and tried to tug her away. 'Lemon? Come on. We need to keep moving. We need to GO!'

'What if she's turned to stone?'

'Don't be ridiculous. LOOK at her!'

Kellogg gently nudged the girl

from the other side while Jake fastened his grip on her trembling forearm and tried to draw her away.

Turning her head slowly, her eyes unfocused. Lemon looked at the other Outcasts as if noticing them for the very first time. Her voice sounded completely distracted.

'Oh, yeah ... sorry. Let's go.'

They moved through the gallery, slipping and sliding on the slanted floor before they practically crashed into the door at the far end of the room.

'Is it locked?' Jake said, trying to stop Rufus from glancing back at the portrait.

'I don't know,' Lemon said, her voice ragged. 'I'm just checking.'

Kellogg tried to move in front of her. 'Can you get it open or not?'

'Just WAIT.'

Lemon grabbed the handle, turned it and pulled. When it didn't budge, she gritted her teeth and yanked so hard that the handle came away, along with a massive sliver of wood and half of the left-hand panel. She tossed the debris aside and flung open the door.

94

7

The Vault

The Outcasts practically fell into the next room, landing on top of each other in an untidy heap. They were a tangle of arms and legs, but they managed to wriggle, crawl and wrestle their way apart before finally finding their feet.

'Er, wow,' said Kellogg, who was the first to stand up.

The Outcasts found themselves in a very large circular room that contained a small island in the middle, surrounded by a deep trench. There was one other door. A strangely powerful light bled down from an unseen source in the ceiling, illuminating something small and square that looked almost exactly like ...

'The box!' Jake said, scrambling onto his feet. 'It is! It's THE box!'

'It can't be!' Lemon exclaimed. 'Fatyak destroyed the box! He hurled the wretched thing off the roof of my house. It must have smashed into a hundred pieces.'

'More,' said Kellogg, pointing at the vast network of hairline cracks and jigsaw shards that adorned the body of the box: these were apparently held together by a glowing white line that might have been some sort of strangely luminescent glue. 'I think there are still parts of it missing, but it looks like it might be, well, functional. I wonder who found all the bits and put them back together.'

'Nathan Heed?'

'I doubt it.'

They gathered around the edge of the trench, Jake peering into the shadows below.

'Strange that you can't see the bottom. I tell you, this house is more than meets the eye. I think we might have rushed into this.'

'I disagree,' Lemon said, glancing

over the side of the trench. 'I say we need answers, a way to stop what's happening to us so we can get our old lives back. How about you, Kellogg?'

The scrawny youth shrugged. 'I don't know. Let's just see what we can find out by sneaking around, then get the hell out of here. I don't know what they've done to Fatyak's mum, but if the statue in the garden *wasn't* her, then we owe it to Fatyak – wherever he is – to do our best to find out what happened.'

Jake shut his eyes and rubbed his head to try to reduce the sharp pain in his temples to a dull ache. When he opened them again, a look of sudden revelation had taken root in his eyes. He was staring directly at the box.

'What if we can give these powers back?' he said. 'I mean *literally* return them to the very THING they came from.'

He didn't say another word, but took several steps back as if he intended to leap the gap.

'What are you doing?' Lemon demanded. 'Don't even think of trying to make a jump like that. You don't have Fatyak's power!'

'I reckon I could make it,' Rufus said. 'I'm smaller than the rest of you, and I was the best long jumper in my year.'

Jake muttered something under

his breath as Lemon and Kellogg both stepped aside to let the boy make a decent run up.

Rufus took a deep breath, crouched down and ran forward. He thundered to the edge of the trench and was just at the point of making the leap when everyone else realised that he wasn't going to make it.

Kellogg tensed, Lemon shut her eyes and Jake shot out a hand, too late.

Rufus went flying over the edge of the trench and cleared the gap before skidding onto the edge of the island. Unfortunately, he had barely landed when the entire lip of the rock split away in a cascade of debris that sent Rufus *plunging* into the dark abyss.

Lemon and Kellogg screamed. Jake closed his eyes to attempt to conjure some magic, but none of them had been expecting the disaster that was playing on in front of them.

⚡

As Rufus fell headlong into the shadows, a million thoughts rushed through his head, the main one being that he couldn't quite believe how far he was falling. He'd firmly expected to hit the bottom of the trench after five or six feet, but the air was rushing up to meet him as if he'd hurled himself off the edge of a cliff.

He tried to scream, but the only sound that left his lips was a wheeze.

Rufus knew with a sudden, terrible certainty that he was going to die. He closed his eyes, braced himself for impact ...

... and froze.

Rufus slowly opened one eye, followed by the other. His face, which had been contorted in preparation for the expected landing, relaxed.

He was hovering above a crackling cloud of blue sparks that was slowly revolving around him to form a makeshift cushion of energy. The sparks fed into a column of sapphire light that funnelled all the way up to the distant light emanating from the chamber far above.

Although he was only suspended for a few seconds before the blue field began to draw him inexorably upwards, Rufus found himself glimpsing the outline of what looked like a vast ruin, *upside down*. It felt as though he were in a scene from Alice in Wonderland. He found himself marvelling at the sheer impossibility of the view.

In the middle of a rocky valley, there stood a collection of ornate but faded pillars and broken statues lining the path towards an archway. Through the archway, sunlight spilt from the far side in molten rays that lit up the inverted cavern. Clearly visible beyond the archway was a temple resplendent in gold, floating on a thick layer of cloud that drifted through the arch and into the cavern on its nearside.

Rufus felt sick from trying to concentrate on this new, alien perspective, but he only had enough to time to gawp at the vista for a few seconds before he was raised up by the growing energy field and deposited back in the box chamber, at the feet of Jake Cherish.

The Outcasts' leader was standing with both arms spread wide. His pupils had rolled back inside his head, leaving white orbs that gave him a completely terrifying appearance as the swirling cloud of blue energy crackled around him.

When Rufus finally came to land, the energy slithered back into Jake's fingertips, like so many wriggling strands of spaghetti.

'Th-thanks, Dealmo!'

Jake nodded. 'Don't mention it.'

'Are you okay?' Lemon said, rushing to the boy's side.

'Yeah,' Kellogg added, crouching

down. 'Do you need healing?'

'N-no, I'm f-fine,' Rufus said, 'listen, though, there's something down there. Something amazing.'

Jake frowned. 'Good amazing or *bad* amazing?'

'An underground chasm of some sort. There's a gate there, like a magic gate. There's sunlight coming out of it and a temple! I think it leads somewhere. Somewhere unimaginable.'

Lemon glanced back towards the portrait room and shuddered.

'I don't want to know,' she said. 'Let's just get the box! If there's even a tiny chance we might be able to reverse what we did ...'

She hurled herself at the trench, leaping over the gap at the last second and landing quite comfortably on the other side.

Then she grabbed the box and lifted it into her arms. As she did so, there was a click from the floor of the little island and a circular pressure plate lifted from the ground.

A deep, booming wail became audible in the chamber. At first, Jake and the other Outcasts thought the resonating sound might be confined to the room and the cavern below, but it soon rose in pitch to become an ear-splitting siren that assaulted the senses.

'Out!' Jake screamed, his voice almost entirely drowned out by the din. 'LEMON! HURRRRY! LET'S! GET! OUUUUUT!'

Clutching the box tightly under one arm, Lemon hurled herself forward, took a thunderous leap from the island and barely cleared the trench. Kellogg snatched out a hand at the last second and dragged her towards him, her boots kicking up a cloud of dust as she scrambled for safety.

The Outcasts bundled into the nearest doorway, practically tumbling over each other as they spilled out into the hall beyond.

Kellogg was the last to cross the threshold, slamming the door behind him.

The alarm ceased immediately, cutting off in the middle of a screeching tone that continued to echo in the ears of The Outcasts for the next few seconds.

'W-where are we?' Rufus said.

The group slowly got to their feet and, glancing around, found that they had arrived in the main hall of Drake Manor, a wide, vaulted room with an enormous, doubled-sided staircase leading to the upper floor.

Jake looked at Rufus. 'This is a trap,' he said, leaving no room for argument. 'I can feel it. Rufus, you are the only one of us who doesn't have some sort of special ability.'

'So? I can still ...'

'NO! Listen to me,' Jake said, his voice harsh with concern. 'I want *you* to take the box from Lemon.'

He waited while the girl handed it over before continuing. 'At the first sign of danger, you HAVE to run. Do you understand? If we get into trouble, you HAVE to get out of here.'

As the smaller boy nodded emphatically, Jake turned to Lemon and Kellogg. 'Right. I guess this is it. Do you two think you can take on The Reach?'

'I don't know.' Lemon admitted, rolled her eyes and pointing an accusatory finger at Jake. 'We should have finished Nathan Heed off when the box was destroyed. If he's meddled with it again, he could turn out to be a real problem for us.'

'I'm afraid that Nathan Heed is the least of your worries,' said a voice from above them.

8

Showdown

All the lights in the manor went on.

Proceeding down the left-hand side of the staircase was an elderly man with a ragged beard, wearing a tarnished tweed jacket. On the right was a young, pale looking boy who was dressed in a strangely unflattering tracksuit, accompanied by a slim, curly haired girl with a pretty face who was wearing a gown that gave off an emerald glow. A writhing, serpentine headdress finished the look that made her seem older than her years.

The old man smiled. 'Welcome, my friends. Welcome to Drake Manor.'

A door flew open and Nathan Heed trudged into the hall, literally clapping his hands with delight. 'I see you've run into a bunch of Outcasts, Sir!' he spat. 'Allow me to help you complete the set!'

'Dealmo, look! They've got Fatyak!'

The giant henchman known as Slud appeared in the doorway, shoving Fatyak in front of him. The boy looked weak and dishevelled. Kellogg ran to help his friend, but Lemon held him back.

'Good work, Nathan,' the old man

continued, turning back to Jake before eyeing the box in Rufus's arms. 'Now, I believe you interfering, meddlesome, spineless little thieves are in possession of a few things that rightfully belong to our *family*. Do you have any idea what happened to the last of your kind who successfully stole from us? What did he take, now ... curse my memory ... *fire*, wasn't it?'

As the boy in the tracksuit nodded, Lemon readied herself for a fight and Kellogg tensed.

Jake stood his ground.

'Are you the leader of The Reach?' he asked, fearful that he already knew the answer. 'Or just another shadowy servant?'

'The Reach? Ah, yes, that's what we're calling ourselves, these days. The colonel's idea, I'm afraid. A very modern man, that one. We are, as you say, *The Reach*. Before that, we were the *New World Order*, which followed *The Illuminated Ones*. I could go on for an hour or more, but, really, what would be the point? It's not as if you're going to be leaving.'

Jake took a deep breath. 'Perhaps, perhaps not. You might find us more difficult to deal with than you think.'

'You want your lightning bolt' Jake

snapped. 'You want all these powers back? That's fine with us, because they've caused us nothing but trouble. You can have them in a heartbeat. Just as soon as you give us Fatyak's mum and let us leave.'

'My *mum?*' Fatyak cried, his eyes frantic with worry. 'What have they done to my mum?'

The old man sneered, his eyes narrowing. 'Don't worry, son,' he said. 'Your mother has never looked better.' He smirked as the boy tried to move forward and found himself yanked back by Slud. Then he turned his attention to Jake.

'I take it you're the leader of this

little group of misfits,' he observed. 'Are you actually *holding* the cylinder with lightning inside yourself? Impressive, very impressive, but I'm afraid it is not yours to bargain with, as the box was not yours to destroy.'

'It wasn't yours either,' Rufus growled. 'The Box belonged to history! It was made by the god Zeus and given to Epimetheus as—'

'... a wedding present' the old man interrupted. 'And what a wedding it was. I remember the look on Pandora's face when I first handed it to her husband: such curiosity, such a burning thirst for *knowledge*. The twin lightning bolts, however, were gifts made specifically for *me*. I still possess one. I understand that *you* now have the other.'

A horrible, deadly silence had taken root in the hall.

'Oh, don't be ridiculous! You're not seriously trying to tell us that you're Zeus!' Lemon smiled nervously, looking to Kellogg for assurance that the old man was joking. 'Zeus doesn't actually EXIST! He's just from an ancient story people used to tell each other! There are no such things as actual *gods*. Not outside of mythology! The box ...'

'The box is real,' Jake muttered, addressing Lemon without taking his eyes off the old man. 'The lightning bolt is real. The gods of the old world were supposed to be cruel and power-hungry. I believe this man *is* Zeus. Or at least, he's what Zeus has *become in immortality.*'

'One chance,' the old man snapped, stepping forward and gripping the banisters so tightly that the wood cracked. 'You have ONE chance. Give me the lightning bolt NOW or I will destroy *all* of you.'

'You want it?' Jake shouted, darting a glance behind him. 'Then come and GET IT!'

Jake turned, shoving Kellogg back

towards Rufus, who had already turned
to flee.

'Run!' he screamed. 'Both of YOU.
RUUUUUUUN!'

9

Battleground

Zeus opened his palm and released a bolt of gleaming light at Jake. The attack was so swift, so sudden, that the boy found himself unable to do anything but stand, open-mouthed, as the searing arrow of energy arced towards him.

Never one to obey instructions, Kellogg leaped in front of his friend and did the first thing that occurred to him. He duplicated the gesture, hurling his own lightning bolt at Zeus. The two blinding forks of energy collided with such force that the chandelier above the hall broke from its moorings, hit the floor and exploded.

The look of horrified shock on the face of Zeus would be burned into Kellogg's memory for the rest of his life.

'YOU!' he boomed, glaring down at the boy with an expression of pure, white hatred. 'YOU have my lightning bolt? How surprising. You don't look strong enough to wield even a *mortal* weapon.'

'Kellogg!' Jake screamed, snatching hold of his friend's t-shirt and yanking him back. 'Follow Rufus! I'm SERIOUS!

Run. Now!'

As his friend finally took notice of the instruction and dashed off along the hall, Jake raised both arms and a swirling cloud of crackling blue energy enveloped him, billowing out around the hall at the foot of the staircase.

'Nathan,' Zeus called, glancing down at Heed. 'This *little boy* appears to be dabbling with *minor* magic. Please teach him the error of his ways.'

'My pleasure, Master,' came the odious reply, but any further comment was abruptly cut off as Lemon charged at Nathan Heed.

Slud ran to intercept the girl, but

Fatyak dived sideways, sliding across the floor and tripping the big man up, who crashed on top of him.

Up on the balcony, Zeus sighed and waved a hand dismissively. Then he called to the youth in the tracksuit. 'Hermes, if you will.'

The boy leaped the banister and landed in front of Jake, who unleashed a jet of black flames upon him. These funnelled into a wide gout of blasting heat that filled the entire hall with thick, curling clouds of smoke.

Nathan Heed braced himself to contain Lemon's wrath, but she cannoned into him at such a speed that the pair of them slid across the floor and crashed through the wall and into the box chamber beyond. She drove a fist at the little man, but he blocked the attempt and started to bend her arm back towards her. They both skidded sideways as they fought for control, their struggle taking them to the very edge of the trench.

Having succeeded in putting Slud on his back, Fatyak seized the initiative and leaped on top of the thug, trying to use his weight to keep him prone. It wasn't easy, but he found strength in the thought that his mum was somewhere in the mansion, trapped and scared. He snarled at Slud, gritted his teeth and drove a flurry of fists at the brute.

Jake's breathtaking flames washed over the Hermes, who had grown in both size and stature and now stood behind a gleaming silver shield that seemed to sprout directly from his hand, while a sword appeared in the other fist. Both artefacts gleamed in a light that seemed all of their own creation, crackling with an energy that Jake thought was very reminiscent of his own magical conjurations.

He continued to send the flames he'd mustered hurtling towards the boy. Yet, when the fires died away, the boy stood unharmed and smiling.

'Is that all you've got, *mortal*?' he spat, flicking out his free hand and conjuring a short sword out of the air. 'Is that all there *is*? Hahaha! What a pathetic assault! You see this shield? It belonged to my older brother, Ares, so it doesn't always obey my commands. This *blade,* on the other hand, has always been solely mine.'

He hurled the sword he was carrying. It spun end over end towards Jake in what seemed like an unstoppable arc, but The Outcasts' leader clapped his hands together and sent the blade clattering harmlessly to the floor in a thin cloud of purple smoke. The look of surprised relief on his face was matched by one of extreme annoyance on the face of his exalted opponent.

'Is that all you've got?' he mimicked, locking eyes with the boy. 'Is that *all there is?*'

Fatyak took a hard slap to the face and tumbled off Slud, rolling a few times and hitting a suit of armour, which came down upon him with a thundering crash.

Cackling with glee, Slud scrambled onto his feet, crossed the hall in two quick strides and dragged Fatyak up by the collar. Lifting the heavy boy high over his head, he surged forward, but the effort was interrupted by a sharp rake across the face as Fatyak's scratchy fingers found the big man's eyes. Slud dropped him immediately, stepping back.

Lemon brought every ounce of her strength to bear against Nathan Heed, who was beginning to buckle under the pressure. She forced the spiteful little man onto his back and over the edge of the trench, but he clung to her frantically, his hands scrambling for purchase on her shirt.

'What's wrong, *Heed*,' Lemon snarled. 'Did you try to use the box again? It doesn't seem to work very well for you, does it? You can't master Dealmo's magic, Kellog's healing or

Fatyak's stealth, but ... you ... think ... you ... can ... overpower ... ME?'

She thrust an open palm into Heed's face, but the little man dodged a second strike and, rolling back over the edge of the trench, cartwheeled sideways, before flipping himself back onto his feet.

'You're right about the magic,' he said, as the cuts on his lips sealed up, 'but I've got the acrobatics and the healing down just fine, *Princess*. Allow me to demonstrate.' He flung out both arms and back-flipped, landing perfectly, and with a wry smile on his face. 'This is the home of the gods, little girl. You're *all* way out of your depth *here*.'

Lemon glared at him, and charged.

Unwittingly, Slud stepped between Jake and the gods, receiving a sword slash up one arm and a sizeable electric shock down the other. He collapsed, and lay still ...

... but the battle in the hall raged on.

10

Fight or Flight

Kellogg thundered along the corridors of Drake Manor, frantically searching for Rufus in every open doorway as he went.

The noise of the battle in the hall was deafening. It seemed to follow him through the house as he hurtled on aimlessly through corridor after corridor, quite certain that he'd passed the same room several times. He skidded to a halt in the middle of a T-junction, his breath fitting and starting in rough bursts, his hand still shaking from the sudden discharge of the lightning bolt.

'Rufus!' he shouted, darting glances left and right. 'Rufus, where are you?'

When he got no reply, Kellogg chose his path at random and plunged along a new hallway full of giant potted plants, slapping away palm-sized fronds as he fought to make his way to the far door.

'Where did you go!'

Kellogg forced open the door, his heart thumping and his head throbbing with a million frantic thoughts. A flood of relief washed over him when he found himself back in the low conservatory with its vast swimming pool and the gentle wash of light that played over the glass ceiling.

There was still no sign of Rufus, however.

Kellogg clapped his hands over his ears to try to block out the distant noise of the battle. Then, his mind awash with the guilt of leaving, he reluctantly dived into the pool and made for the tunnel that fed into the gardens.

Carving through the water with every ounce of weary strength he had left, Kellogg could think only of getting away and how much it felt like he was letting his friends down.

He knew Jake was right: the lightning bolt might belong to the ancient, cold-hearted god, but it was too dangerous to be handed back to him.

I'll get it as far away from the manor as I can, he thought, *and then I'll come back for my friends.* But he knew deep down that The Outcasts would do just fine as a trio. They'd never needed him for anything more than a bit of minor healing. Not really.

He dragged himself from the narrow pool. And a boot stamped down on his hand.

'Arghhhhh!'

'Well, if it isn't young Mr Kellogg,'

said Colonel Bleach, reaching down to drag the scrawny youth to his feet. 'And where would you be going in such a hurry?'

He smiled humourlessly, flipped Kellogg onto his back and dragged him across the garden.

'L-l-let go of me!'

'I don't think so, you little coward,' Bleach mumbled, snatching hold of Kellogg flailing right leg and twisting it cruelly to one side.

'Arghhgh!'

Feeling his bone begin to break, the boy drove his fist forward and released a bolt of lightning that missed Bleach's head by no more than a few inches.

The colonel relinquished his grip on Kellogg and took up a defensive stance as the angry youth clambered to his feet.

'Not really fair, is it?' Bleach growled, raising his fists and clenching them until the knuckles turned white. 'I mean, you're armed with a deadly weapon and I'm fighting in the traditional way, the way any *real* man would fight: hand to hand.'

Before Kellogg could respond, Bleach crossed the distance between them and caught him with a kick that completely winded him. As he doubled up, the colonel reached down and shoved him back onto the ground with a minimum of effort.

'Pathetic,' he yelled. 'Completely and utterly pathetic. I've fought small children who've put up a better defence than you.'

He prodded the boy with his boot.

'You seemed much braver when you were electrocuting me back at the museum' he said. 'I suppose you need your friends a bit more than they need you.'

Kellogg screamed and kicked out with a sweep of his leg, but Bleach saw the move coming and leaped over the limb, driving down a foot as he landed.

'Arghghgh!' Kellogg coughed, rolling into a foetal position and hugging his legs.

'Get up,' the colonel whispered, snatching hold of the boy's hair and hauling him onto his feet. 'Now, let's see what you can do.'

He shoved the youth backwards and returned to a defensive position, raising his arms once again as if he were about to enter a boxing match. 'Come at me, you pitiful wretch.'

Kellogg said nothing. He simply raised his arm, closed one eye and sighted Bleach along the limb. 'I've always hated fighting,' he said. 'My dad used to tell me that the best thing to do in a fight was just to turn and walk away.'

Bleach snorted. 'Your dad sounds like a coward,' he said.

Kellogg took a deep breath, and swallowed. 'You've picked a fight with a skinny kid who hates fighting,' he said. 'I've done nothing but help people with *my power. You're* the coward.'

Bleach clapped his hands with glee. 'Tough talk. Well, unlike your *cowardly* father, I'm not going to *let* you walk away. So, you're going to *have* to try to defend yourself.'

He lunged at the boy. But Kellogg ran.

Feeling nothing but an acute awareness of his own fear, Kellogg almost collided with the first statue in the stone garden, and then, turning back to face Bleach, began to retreat among the frozen figures.

Colonel Bleach stalked his prey like a tiger, moving in slow, deliberate strides.

'See these ornaments?' he yapped. 'They were all people, once. You'll recognise a few of them, I'm sure: your friend's mother, the sad little chap who ran the game shop. A few them are from your time, some lived a long time before you or friends were anything more than future echoes. A pity you can't use your dainty little healing hands on this mob, eh?'

As Bleach spoke, Kellogg realised that he had a hand on each statue. His eyes found the paralysed faces of Stew Butter and Mrs Reed. The idea of using his gift had never even occurred to him.

Closing his eyes, he ignored the advance of Colonel Bleach and tightly shut his eyes, feeling the familiar flood of warmth birthing in his stomach and washing up through his body until the tide of light energy sailed down either arm.

From somewhere far beyond the reach of audible noise, Kellogg detected a tiny shift in reality. When he opened his eyes, he was still staring at the same frozen expressions, but he watched the lips of the statues begin to move and murmurings of speech could be heard.

'Wh-what happened?' said Butter.

'Where's my Fernando?' said Mrs Reed.

Colonel Bleach dashed forward and Kellogg hit him full in the chest with a lightning bolt.

The discharge on the bolt was short, sudden and explosive, and the force of the impact took Colonel Bleach off his feet and spun him through three hundred and sixty degrees in the air, before depositing him hard on the turf.

⚡

Lemon hurled Nathan Heed against the wall of the trench chamber, hiking up a kick that she used to spear the little man in place, her heel pinning him by the shoulder.

'It's over, Nathan,' she said, tired but confident now she had the upper hand. 'I don't want to hurt you, but I absolutely will with no hesitation if you don't take this one chance to go.'

'Ha!' Heed swiped ineffectually at the girl's leg, but couldn't dislodge the foot from his shoulder. 'You must be insane, child. I report to the *gods*. Don't you understand that? The very *gods* themselves. You can't honestly think you'll win *here*.'

Lemon shrugged, released her grip on Heed and took several steps back, until she stood with her feet on the lip of the trench. 'Go home, Nathan,' she said. 'Find whatever rock you crawled out from, and slither back under it.'

Nathan Heed cackled with demented glee ... and charged.

Lemon stepped aside at the last second, spinning with such force that the back of her left elbow propelled Heed over the edge of the trench and into the chasm below.

His screams seemed to last an age before they gave way to a deathly silence.

⚡

As Colonel Bleach tried and failed to get to his feet, Kellogg made an effort to steer Stew Butter and Fatyak's mother away from the stone garden.

'I still don't understand. W-what's going on?'

'Are all these other people ...'

'Where's my son?'

'Both of you! Just listen to me,' Kellogg shouted. 'Get as far away from here as possible. Take the main road, get into town and call the police. Just tell them Fatyak, I mean Fernando, has been taken hostage by a gang. Do you understand?'

'My boy! My poor boy!'

'He'll be okay,' Kellogg said, patting her affectionately on the arm with a vaguely confused expression on his face. 'I'm sure everything will be fine once you get to the police station.'

Kellogg propelled them both towards the main gate before he returned to the stone garden.

Colonel Bleach was nowhere to be seen.

Kellogg moved cautiously between the statues, wondering whether to resurrect them, and then remembering that some of them had probably been statues for a very long time. A lot more thought would be required before any rash decisions could be made.

Kellogg moved up and down the rows, carefully studying each statue in the shadowy light, until suddenly one of the taller ones darted out an arm and practically garrotted him.

'I'm not done with you yet, boy,' Bleach threatened, flexing his muscles and patting his charred shirt. 'Not by a long shot.'

He reached down to pick the boy off the ground, and Kellogg surprised himself by knocking the man unconscious with a single punch that contained every ounce of strength he had left.

They both crashed to the ground before Kellogg began, very slowly, to crawl away.

11

The Last Stand

'Enough!' Zeus flew over the gallery banister and took the stairs three at a time, his vast strides seeming grotesque in the elderly human body he was occupying. 'We will end this. NOW!'

Grabbing Hermes and tossing his own son aside like a rag doll, he swung out a wild arm, spewing forth an icy wind that hurled the remaining Outcasts against the far wall.

'Don't think we're ungrateful for the

entertainment,' Zeus boomed, as Hermes made a determined effort to get back on his feet, 'but the novelty has worn off. You and your friends have most definitely outstayed your welcome here.'

The Outcasts leaned heavily on each other, battered and bruised and now freezing cold from the ordeal. Turning tired eyes to his friend, Jake Cherish coughed and slapped a hand on Fatyak's shoulder.

'Are we ready to give in, Yakker?' he said. 'Should we hold up our hands in defeat, let theses gods roll right over us? They *are* immortal, after all.'

'Who cares?' Fatyak spat,

massaging his wrist while clenching and unclenching the other hand. 'I think we've got one more round in us, Dealmo,' he added. 'Let's go out fighting.'

Jake grinned, manically. 'Your call, dude.'

He spun round, threw up a hand and concentrated on the wall of the hallway, where several rows of decorative, ceremonial knives hung, each one supported by a heavily reinforced wooden bracket.

As he focused all of his attention on the wall, a number of the knives began to rattle in their holdings, pre-empting a series of loud cracks as the wooden supports sheared in half. All at once, a hurricane of blades took to the air.

Zeus glanced upwards, snarling as the knives rained down on him. But Hermes flew across the room, holding up the oblong shield which immediately expanded into a wide dome of protection.

Jake watched as the knives flew into the surface of the dome, effectively turning the shield into a giant pin cushion.

Looking irritated, Hermes muttered an incantation and, waiting a few seconds for the shield to return to its usual size, hurled the blade-sprouting oblong directly at The Outcasts.

Fatyak pushed Jake aside and

somersaulted backwards. The shield crashed into the staircase, exploding through the banisters before ending its journey in the wall.

Hermes waited for Fatyak to spring back to his feet, then flew forward as if he'd been propelled out of a cannon. He landed directly in front of the biggest Outcast, throwing a sharp punch ...

... which narrowly missed its target.

Fatyak dodged back, beckoning the younger god forward.

'Is it true,' he said. 'You know, everything I read about you in school? The sneaking around, the evil tricks, the winged sandals?'

Hermes aimed a second strike at Fatyak: this one grazed the boy, but was still wide of the mark.

'These are Boots of Leaping,' Hermes cackled, conversationally. 'Not quite as obvious as the sandals, but far better for blending in when you're food shopping.'

He struck out with a third blow, but telegraphed the move so obviously that Fatyak dodged aside with seconds to spare, slapping the god with all his might on the back of the neck.

Hermes staggered forward, boiling with furious anger and humiliation. There was a deep pink handprint on the surface of his skin.

'He struck you!' Zeus exclaimed, an edge of disgust in his voice. 'This rotund youngling actually managed to lay a finger on YOU?'

He bunched up a fist and fired an elongated lightning bolt at Fatyak.

Sensing that his friend didn't have the energy to dodge it, Jake poured all his own energy into generating an electric shield to stop the bolt, but the sheer strength of the weapon was overwhelming: it crashed into the temporary barrier with an explosion that sent both him and Fatyak flying off in different directions.

Jake hit the wall, hard.

Fatyak went through an ornate cabinet in a shattering shower of glass.

Then, silence.

'Mortals,' said Zeus, in a condescending tone. 'They get hold of the smallest glimmer of power, and they presume to challenge the very *heavens* with it, like so many ants trying to carry the weight of the world.' He glanced sharply at his son. 'They've seen far too much. Return their power to the box and finish them off.'

'My pleasure, Father.'

Hermes nodded, bowed low and pranced theatrically across the hallway ...

... but he found his route blocked by Lemon.

The girl was battered and badly bruised, but, if anything, she looked stronger and more determined than ever.

'Your friend Nathan Heed took a shortcut to the basement,' she said. 'Care to join him?'

⚡

Dazed, confused and exhausted from his battle with Colonel Bleach, Kellogg dashed across the garden and wriggled through the generous gap Lemon had made in the fence.

Lemon.

As he ran, Kellogg began to feel tears leaking from his eyes.

They have to win, he thought. *They have to. Please let them win.*

He ran up the hill in the moonlight, his cheeks wet and his chest heaving with sobs of despair.

'I'm sorry,' he said aloud, looking back at the floodlit house and its garden of stone statues. 'I'm so, so sorry.'

He took one final glance at the rooftop battlements of Drake Mansion ...

... and saw Rufus crouched on the highest turret.

⚡

Lemon closed a fist around Hermes' wiry hand, lifted the young god into the air and hurled him as hard as she could towards the staircase.

Zeus casually stepped aside, his son stopping some way from the stairs and hovering on the air.

'It's not easy to harm us,' the old god laughed. 'Many have attempted it, more have failed.'

'I'm not trying to hurt you,' Lemon admitted, helping Jake and Fatyak to their feet. 'I'm trying to buy us some time to regroup.'

'I think not.' Zeus smiled, but his face settled into an odd grimace. He snapped his fingers and the girl in the green dress, who had been silently watching the battle without making the slightest move to get involved, skipped down from the staircase, a playful smile on her lips. She reached a hand to her face and very carefully removed her sunglasses.

Fatyak, Jake and Lemon took defensive positions and readied themselves for another attack, but the girl simply smiled and then focused the full force of her unearthly gaze on the three of them.

'What the ...' Fatyak froze, his

eyes wide and his hands dropping to his sides.

Mere feet away from him, Jake helplessly duplicated the action.

Both friends took several steps toward the girl, almost stumbling into each other in their hurry to reach her.

She smiled, put a gentle hand on the shoulder of each boy and fastened them with a glance that she quickly switched from one to the other. She was so strikingly beautiful that her face seemed to shine as if she was being illuminated by a spotlight.

'Ssssssssssssstop ssssssstruggling,' she sang out a beautifully melodious tone. In the blink of an eye, she turned both Jake and Fatyak to stone.

Lemon tried to cry out, but her voice was dry and all she could see were those terrible emerald eyes filling her entire field of vision. She took several steps back, but the girl seemed to swim towards her in a strange, swaying motion that turned the entire room into a giant whirlpool.

Lemon gasped, and found herself unable to move.

As her skin solidified, her mouth was captured in a terrible, permanent rictus.

'Very good, my dear,' the old

god boomed. 'Now let us take these new fascinating new additions into the garden. Colonel Bleach is on watch duty tonight, so I doubt the other two little thieves can have wandered very far.'

⚡

On the roof of the tallest tower at Drake Manor, Rufus crouched down, opened the box and placed his hand over the palm print that had been inlaid on the underside of the lid.

'I know what I want,' he said. 'I know exactly who I've always wanted to be. Y-you can give that to me, right? You can m-make it happen?'

He looked down at the box, which began – very slowly – to glow.

⚡

Kellogg cupped his hands around his mouth and took a deep breath. He was about to shout at the distant figure of Rufus when his attention was unexpectedly captured by something that was happening in the floodlit grounds of the house.

The old man who had claimed to be Zeus led his two companions in the direction of the stone garden. Kellogg felt his heart begin to thump loudly in his chest as his eyes searched the shadows frantically for any sign of his friends.

Then he saw them.

Floating on a small cushion of clouds that were apparently being supplied by the petulant-looking boy, the three Outcasts were all frozen in the same helpless positions, their skin grey and lifeless. From where Kellogg was standing, he couldn't see if they were merely paralysed or actually turned to stone, but they were all quickly deposited on the hard ground with what definitely sounded like a heavy 'thunk'.

I can save them, he thought. *If I can just get close enough, I can save them.*

Kellogg hunkered down on the hill, crouching as the group in the garden began to spread out across the grounds, apparently searching for something elsewhere, something illusive.

His hands beginning to shake with fear, Kellogg returned his attention to the topmost turret of the manor. But Rufus had disappeared.

Kellogg frowned. *Where did he go?*

He scanned the entire rooftop, looking for any sign that the small boy had either fallen from his perch or was running along the stark battlements, but Rufus was nowhere to be seen.

Wherever you are, little guy, Kellogg thought, *I really hope you don't try to do anything stupid.*

'Don't worry, I won't.'

Kellogg practically jumped out of his skin when he saw Rufus standing next to him, the box wedged firmly under one arm.

'What the ...'

'You okay?'

'How did ...'

'Is that the others down there? Oh no! They've been turned to stone! They must be so scared. Let me concentrate for a second!' He tightly shut his eyes, as if he had a terrible headache that he was trying to subdue.

'Where the hell did you come from?'

'The roof.'

'You can't possibly have climbed down that quickly: I just *saw* you up there!'

Rufus sniffed, putting down his burden and rubbing his forehead with the back of one hand. 'I used the box,' he said, crouching to tuck the ancient artefact under one of the thick, rambling bushes that grew from the hillside.

'You did WHAT?'

'Don't worry,' the small boy said excitedly, clapping his hands. 'I knew exactly what to wish for, because I once saw this brilliant show where the hero could—'

'THAT BOX IS NOT A TOY,' Kellogg growled, grabbing Rufus by the arm to get his attention. 'The others are all in terrible danger. This is not a game. Jake told us to *run*.'

'*You* didn't get very far!' Rufus smiled up at him. 'Besides, it's a good job *neither of us* listened to Dealmo. Because we *can* help them now. I saw you from the roof when you unfroze Fatyak's mum and that strange guy with all the hair.'

Kellogg just stared at Rufus, as if noticing for the first time how young he was.

'In case you haven't noticed, there are three immortals standing between us and our friends,' he said, his voice a weak tremor.

'Yeah, agreed,' said Rufus. 'But you've got lightning bolts and I can teleport to any location and read minds!'

Kellogg felt his jaw drop and his eyebrows raise. 'You can WHAT?'

Rufus beamed at him. 'I'm the Great Rodundo!' he shouted, flinging out his arms. 'You know, from the TV show? The Great Rodundo and his sidekick, Chives!'

'You shouldn't have done this, Rufus,' Kellogg said sadly. 'You're too young to control these powers. And I can't even *use* the ligthning bolt properly. I had to knock Bleach out with a *punch*.'

Rufus shrugged.

'I might just seem like an excited little kid right now, but I probably know more about Greek gods *and* superheroes than any of you. I know what powers work best together, and how to use them against evil. Oh, and I'll tell you something you *don't* know. The old god down there is really frightened that you're going to figure out how to *charge up your lightning bolt*. So, I'm guessing you just need to concentrate more. Now, listen ...' he looked up at Kellogg with a very serious expression on his face. 'I'd like to take charge here and I have a pretty great plan. I need to go back into the house to fetch something, but if you do exactly what I say, I'm confident that we can save *everyone*. Are you in?'

Kellogg gawped at the boy, but found himself saying, 'I'm in.'

12

Game Over

'Father! Look!'

Zeus turned to see where his son was pointing and raised an eyebrow as Kellogg stepped between the bent railings and walked across the garden towards them. The scrawny youth was holding one arm behind his back as if he'd been injured.

'It's the boy who has your lightning bolt,' Hermes chuckled, evilly. 'It seems he found his courage after all. Should I go look for the younger one who has our box?'

Zeus shook his head. 'First things first.' He glanced across the stone garden to the spot where Colonel Bleach was lying, his eyes closed and his chest rising and falling in great, heaving sighs. 'Did you do that?' he asked. 'Very impressive, I must say. Bleach is one of my best lieutenants; he's a very competent fighter. Perhaps you aren't quite the stringy runt you so closely resemble.'

Kellogg said nothing, but came to a halt in front of the group.

'What do they call you, boy?'

'Kellogg,' said Kellogg.

'Well, you made the right decision, Kellogg,' Zeus boomed. 'Now, if you simply hold out your hand and allow me to draw the lightning from you, I will make what follows as painless as I can.'

Kellogg nodded, but didn't move an inch.

As Hermes and the girl gleefully gathered round, Zeus strode up to him and forwarded an outstretched hand with fingertips that glowed a deep orange.

'Do it,' the god boomed. 'Do it NOW.'

Kellogg swallowed, produced an arm from behind his back that shone molten yellow and fired a lightning bolt that sent the old god through six of the manor's walls before he came to rest on the precipice of the trench.

The explosion was deafening.

Kellogg leaped back and gritted his teeth. 'Who's next?'

Starting in shock, Hermes took to the air and soared after his father, ducking under the crumbling outer wall of the mansion as he tried to reach the fallen god.

The girl gave a smile that curled her lips and stepped directly in front of Kellogg, her eyes fixed on him.

There was a flash and Rufus appeared between them, holding a mirror right in front of her face.

Medusa's mouth contorted into a terrified scream as she caught sight of her own reflection. And then she froze.

Every statue in the garden came to life.

⚡

Fatyak, Lemon and Jake staggered around the garden between a hoard of equally disorientated people who looked like extras in a historical TV drama. It took them several seconds to find each other before Kellogg located *them*.

'Rufus used the box,' he said,

pointing at the only stone statue now occupying the garden. 'He stopped Medusa and saved you all.'

'Where's my mum?' Fatyak yelled, cradling his head as a spasm of pain shot up his neck. 'I can't see her anywhere. Is she okay?'

'She's FINE,' Kellogg assured him. 'I sent her and Stew Butter off to get the police.'

Jake shook his head, wincing as the movement felt strange after the experience of being frozen. 'Where is Rufus now?'

Kellogg peered around. 'I don't know! He can teleport, though!'

Lemon and Fatyak shared a glance.

'He can WHAT?'

'Don't worry about it. Let's just find him!'

Fatyak thrust out a hand and snatched hold of Kellogg's shirt. 'We'll find him alright,' he said. 'But first, tell me something. Where's the BOX?'

⚡

Hermes came to land beside his father, snatching out a hand to steady the older god as he scrambled away from the edge of the trench.

'We'll wipe them out,' he promised. 'We'll destroy *all* of them. We can't let these mortals make fools of us.'

In another blinding flash, Rufus appeared behind the young god, snatched at his legs and tipped him over. Then he yanked the leather boots from Hermes' feet, before tossing them into the trench.

'Not so flighty without these, are you?' he quipped, before vanished again, just after Hermes leaped to his feet and drove a fist at his back.

But Hermes' punch glanced off the chin of his father, who staggered back with a stunned look on his face.

'F-father!' Hermes exclaimed. 'I-I'm sorry!'

Zeus clenched his teeth and glared at his son, but before he could reply, Rufus appeared behind Hermes and pushed him over the edge of the trench.

'Arghghgh!'

Zeus made to spring forward after his son, but then had second thoughts and stood deathly still, his eyes closing and smoke spilling from his nostrils. Muttering under his breath, he vanished.

There was a flash and Rufus appeared next to the exact spot Zeus had been standing.

The boy looked around and behind

him, but the old god was nowhere to be seen. Rufus concentrated on another shift, but Zeus manifested right in front of him and seized him by the throat.

'Not so quick now, are you?' the old god boomed, lifting Rufus off his feet and holding the boy aloft, his legs flailing madly in the air. 'You'll find it exceptionally difficult to teleport while you're fighting for breath.'

'He won't need to teleport,' said a voice.

Zeus dropped Rufus and stepped back.

He was surrounded by The Outcasts. Fatyak had leaped the trench with comparative ease, the box clutched in his arms. Lemon had the statue of Medusa raised above her head and Kellogg was aiming one blazing yellow arm at Zeus' head.

'It's over,' said Jake, moving between his friends with a trail of blue energy flowing out around him. He came to a halt beside Rufus. 'We've fought you to a standstill, the police are on their way and you've got a crowd of confused victims who look like they're from the history channel wandering around in the garden, looking for answers.'

He allowed the energy to flood through him, dyeing his eyes a brilliant blue. 'Now, I'm sure your son is fine, and even Colonel Bleach. I know we can't destroy any of you — not really — and those other thugs will probably live to fight another day. But, I also know you've kept your entire existence here a well-guarded secret.' He folded his arms and stared the god directly in the eye. 'Tell us how to return our powers to the box, take it back along with your gorgon girl and your precious lightning and leave this place. We've seen the gate, so we know you can come and go where you please. Just don't come back HERE.'

Zeus stared with cold, hollow eyes at the implacable face of Jake Cherish.

Then, almost imperceptibly, he gave a nod.

Lemon stepped forward, depositing the statue of Medusa before the old god, while Kellogg reduced the pressure in his arm and offered a reluctant hand to Zeus.

The old god reached out and took hold of the hand, a molten yellow glow signalling the transfer between them. Jake, Lemon, Fatyak and Rufus steeled themselves for any sudden, expected betrayal, but the transfer completed and Zeus stepped back.

As the distant sound of police sirens alerted them to the arrival of the authorities, Zeus turned to Fatyak and raised an arm.

'Place your hand inside the lid of the box and think about your life before you found it,' he said, simply. 'Any memory will do.'

'Th-that's it?' said Fatyak, his voice full of disappointment. 'No magic words? No giant guardians to defeat? Just *memories*?'

'Yes.'

Zeus gave a dispassionate shrug, but a nod from Jake instructed Fatyak to make the gesture.

The Outcasts watched as Fatyak took a sudden leap and crossed the expansive trench with comparative ease. 'What?' he said, glancing around at them, accusingly. 'Well, I won't be able to do it afterwards, will I?'

He plunged a hand into the box, closed his eyes and *remembered*. There were no lights, no crackles of energy, not even the slightest noise. Yet, somehow, after a few seconds, Fatyak seemed to deflate without actually becoming any smaller. It was as though the shadows around him began to shorten.

He looked up from the box with a sigh and they all knew that his magical abilities were gone. One by one, the other Outcasts followed: Lemon, Kellogg and Rufus (who was very reluctant to let go of his brand new skills.)

Finally, Jake Cherish stepped up to the box and performed his own ceremony of remembrance before handing it back to the old god.

'I have your word that you will leave this place and not return?' he asked, depositing the magic artefact in the hands of its creator.

Zeus nodded and, magically raising the statue of Medusa to float beside him, crossed the room to stand on the very edge of the trench.

Just before he jumped into the chasm, he turned and nodded a final farewell to The Outcasts.

'Jake Cherish,' he said, reflectively. 'We shall watch the progress of your life with great interest.'

Then, all at once, he was gone.

Epilogue

The Outcasts sat on the rough brick wall opposite Stew Butter's game shop, watching as the last of the gaming tables were unceremoniously loaded into the big removal van.

'You think the detectives ever got through with all those interviews?' Fatyak laughed. 'I've never seen so many dazed and confused people in one police station.'

'I heard a sergeant say he thought

it was a big LARPing group who'd had too much to drink,' Lemon said, adding 'Live Action Roleplaying,' when Rufus looked confused. 'Fatyak, how's your mum?'

'Yeah ... she still doesn't really have a clue what happened. She just thinks the house got broken into and they knocked her unconscious.'

'Better than being told you were frozen by Medusa and a bunch of Greek gods who wanted their toys back,' Kellogg laughed.

The group sat in silence for a while as the last of Butter's merchandise was brought out through the little doorway.

'It's the end of an era,' Jake said,

sounding stronger than he felt. 'The note on the window says it's going to be a coffee shop.'

'Like the world needs more of them,' Kellogg muttered. 'My mum said there are three different chains right next door to each other at the shopping centre. I just don't understand it.'

'It's like the bookshops,' Lemon added. 'Loads of people walk through them just to get to the café upstairs.'

'We'll end up in a world with loads of coffee, but no books or games,' Jake moped. 'What a horrible thought.'

'There's still the Dungeons and Dragons club at School,' Fatyak reminded them. 'It starts up again this Friday, remember?'

Kellogg and Lemon stared blankly at him.

'A mobile hut full of fifth years pretending to be hobbits?' Jake laughed. 'I think I'll join you on Xbox LIVE.'

'Now just hold on a minute,' said a familiar voice, as Stew Butter climbed off an ancient looking mountain bike that he proceeded to park up beside them. 'Dungeons and Dragons is no joke. I remember when ...'

'We've heard all the stories a thousand times,' Jake reminded him, sliding across the wall to make a space for the man to sit down. 'But we are sorry about the game shop. It was a great place to hang out. The best ever, actually.'

Stew smiled beneficently. 'It certainly was,' he said. 'You shouldn't stop playing games just because we're closing down, though.' He stared wistfully at the shop front, where two carpenters were clearly visible in the window, sawing at either end of a big workbench. 'In fact, I've got this brand new one on order from Kickstarter which is supposed to be unlike anything you've ever seen before. The leaflet says it's so realistic that you, well, you really *feel* like you're the heroes. Oh, but I suppose, I mean I guess you lot must … well … you know.'

He trailed off, noticing that all five Outcasts were staring at him with expressions of frank astonishment.

'Yeah, Stew,' said Jake Cherish, finally. 'All things considered, I think that — after the last game you sold us — we'll just take our chances with online gaming for a bit.'

As Stew got back on his bike and cycled over to the small gathering of businessmen outside the shop, Lemon heaved a despondent sigh.

'All the kids plays online, nowadays,' she said. 'Do we really want to be like everyone else?'

'I know,' Fatyak snapped. 'Especially since we've effectively just been through one giant video game ourselves. That creepy house with all the rooms was definitely the bonus round. And Zeus was one mother of an end of level boss!'

'Exactly,' said Kellogg, winking at Fatyak and patting Rufus on the shoulder. 'I preferred it when we were just the ordinary sort of outcasts.'

Jake laughed and gave a defeated shrug. 'Hey,' he said. 'No matter what games we play, we'll *always* be The Outcasts.'

He gave Kellogg, Fatyak, Lemon

and Rufus a series of high fives, and headed home.

THE END

ACKNOWLEDGMENTS

I'd like to thank Polly Lyall Grant for her tireless efforts on the Outcasts series. We were shortlisted for the Portsmouth Book Award at the end of 2016, the first time I've ever been shortlisted for anything. Thanks also to the dynamic duo of my ongoing career: Sophie Hicks and Anne McNeil.

REVIEWS

"I love outcasts because it's about kids who are different: Jake and lemon are my favourite characters. I think they are both a little bit like me."

NINA, AGE 8

"The Outcasts is one of those books where you can't stop yourself turning the page!"

GUY, AGE 10

"I felt I was actually inside the story and not just reading it"

RAFE, AGE 10

"It has a lot of cool action!"

JAMES, AGE 9